Graphic

GREAT
EXPECTATIONS

Retold by Hilary Burningham
Illustrated by Chris Rowlatt

Evans

For Atticus

Published in 2009 by Evans Brothers Ltd
2A Portman Mansions
Chiltern St
London W1U 6NR

British Library Cataloguing in Publication Data

Burningham, Hilary.
Great expectations. -- (Graphic Dickens)
    1. England--Social conditions--19th century--Comic books,
    strips, etc.--Juvenile fiction. 2. Bildungsromans.
    3. Children's stories--Comic books, strips, etc.
    I. Title II. Series III. Rowlatt, Chris. IV. Dickens,
    Charles, 1812-1870.
    741.5-dc22

ISBN: 9780237536220

Editor: Bryony Jones
Designer: Mark Holt

MY NAME IS PHILIP PIRRIP, BUT I CALL MYSELF PIP. EXCEPT FOR MY SISTER, MY FAMILY ARE ALL DEAD. SOMETIMES I VISIT THEIR GRAVES.

Keep still, you little devil, or I'll cut your throat!

Don't cut my throat, sir, pray don't do it, sir!

Where's your mother and father?

In those graves, sir. I live with my sister, sir - Mrs Joe Gargery. Joe is the blacksmith.

A blacksmith, eh? Early tomorrow morning, you bring me a file and some food. You bring 'em to me or I'll have your heart and liver out. I have a friend who'll see to it.

An escaped prisoner! I must do as he says.

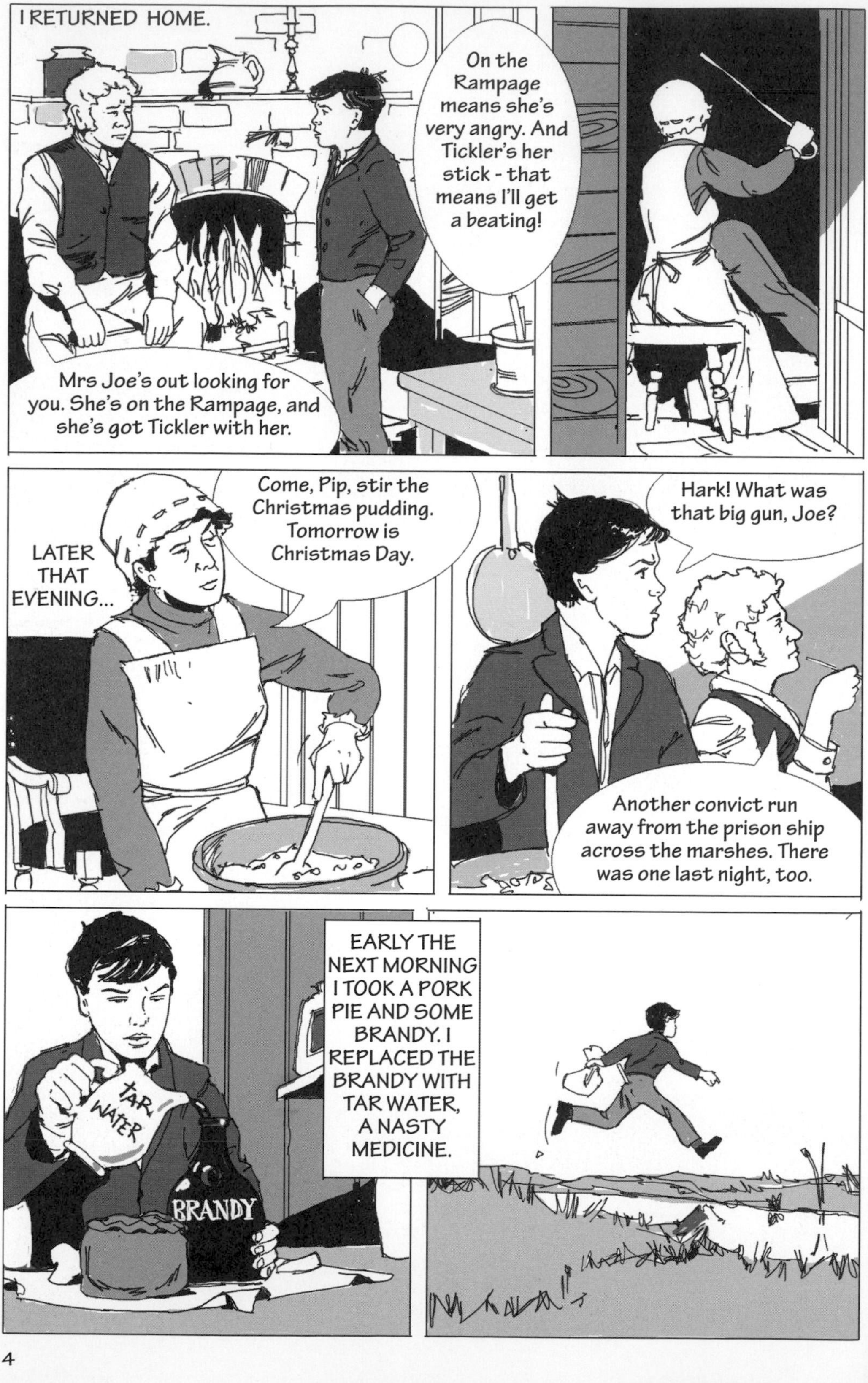
I RETURNED HOME.
Mrs Joe's out looking for you. She's on the Rampage, and she's got Tickler with her.
On the Rampage means she's very angry. And Tickler's her stick - that means I'll get a beating!
LATER THAT EVENING...
Come, Pip, stir the Christmas pudding. Tomorrow is Christmas Day.
Hark! What was that big gun, Joe?
Another convict run away from the prison ship across the marshes. There was one last night, too.
TAR WATER
BRANDY
EARLY THE NEXT MORNING I TOOK A PORK PIE AND SOME BRANDY. I REPLACED THE BRANDY WITH TAR WATER, A NASTY MEDICINE.

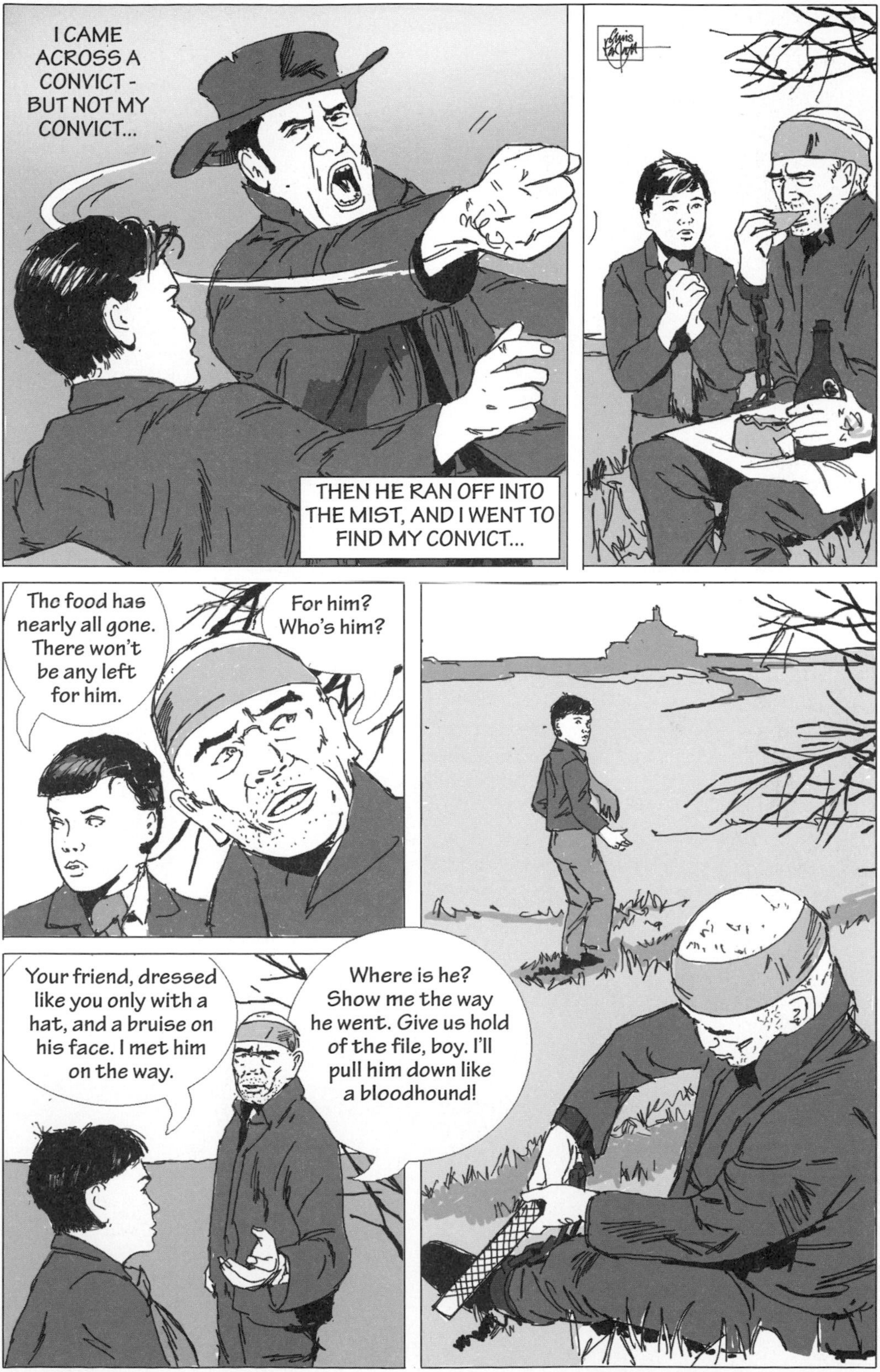
I CAME ACROSS A CONVICT - BUT NOT MY CONVICT...
THEN HE RAN OFF INTO THE MIST, AND I WENT TO FIND MY CONVICT...
The food has nearly all gone. There won't be any left for him.
For him? Who's him?
Your friend, dressed like you only with a hat, and a bruise on his face. I met him on the way.
Where is he? Show me the way he went. Give us hold of the file, boy. I'll pull him down like a bloodhound!

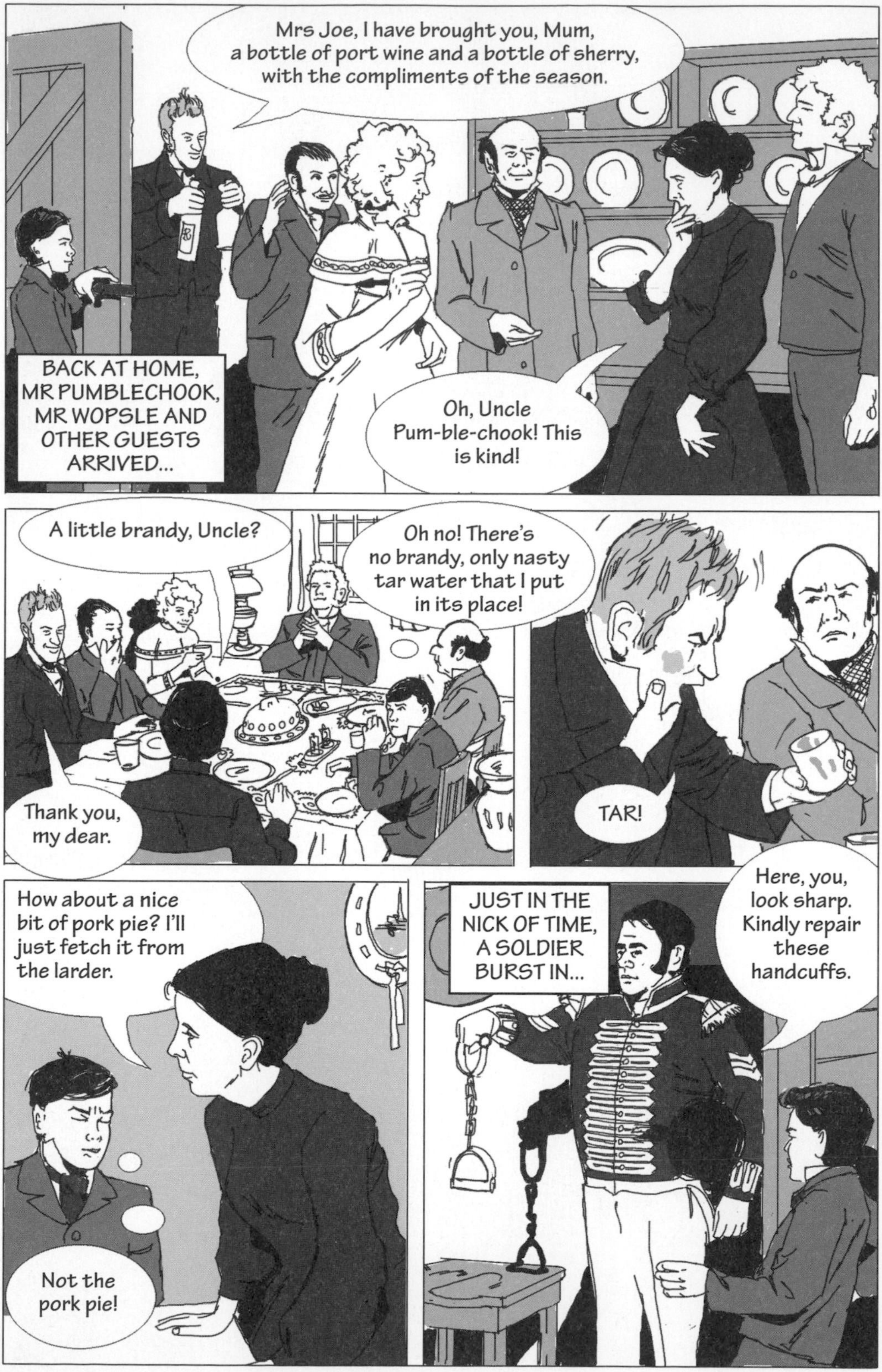
Mrs Joe, I have brought you, Mum, a bottle of port wine and a bottle of sherry, with the compliments of the season.
BACK AT HOME, MR PUMBLECHOOK, MR WOPSLE AND OTHER GUESTS ARRIVED...
Oh, Uncle Pum-ble-chook! This is kind!
A little brandy, Uncle?
Thank you, my dear.
Oh no! There's no brandy, only nasty tar water that I put in its place!
TAR!
How about a nice bit of pork pie? I'll just fetch it from the larder.
Not the pork pie!
JUST IN THE NICK OF TIME, A SOLDIER BURST IN...
Here, you, look sharp. Kindly repair these handcuffs.

May we come with you to search for the convicts? I'd like to see these fellows caught.

MR WOPSLE, JOE AND I WENT TO THE MARSHES...

Murder! Convicts! Runaways!

This way - we've got 'em!

THE TWO CONVICTS WERE FIGHTING EACH OTHER...

7

THE TWO CONVICTS WERE ROWED BACK TO THE PRISON SHIPS.

You're to stay at Uncle Pumblechook's house tonight, and he'll take you there in the morning. Come here - let's clean you up.

Uncle Pumblechook says that Miss Havisham, the rich old lady who lives in the big house, wants a boy to go and play there. That's you, Pip.

Goodbye, Joe.

God bless you, Pip, old chap.

MR PUMBLECHOOK LED ME TO THE GATES OF THE HOUSE.

This is Pip, is it? Come in, Pip.

Behave yourself here, Pip.

Who is it?

I am very sorry, I can't play just now, Miss Havisham.

Then call Estella. You can do that.

Pip, Miss Havisham. Mr Pumblechook's boy, Ma'am. Come to play.

Good. Then play.

Call Estella, at the door.

Estella, let me see you play cards with this boy.

With this boy? Why, he is a common, working boy!

What coarse hands he has, this boy! And what thick boots.

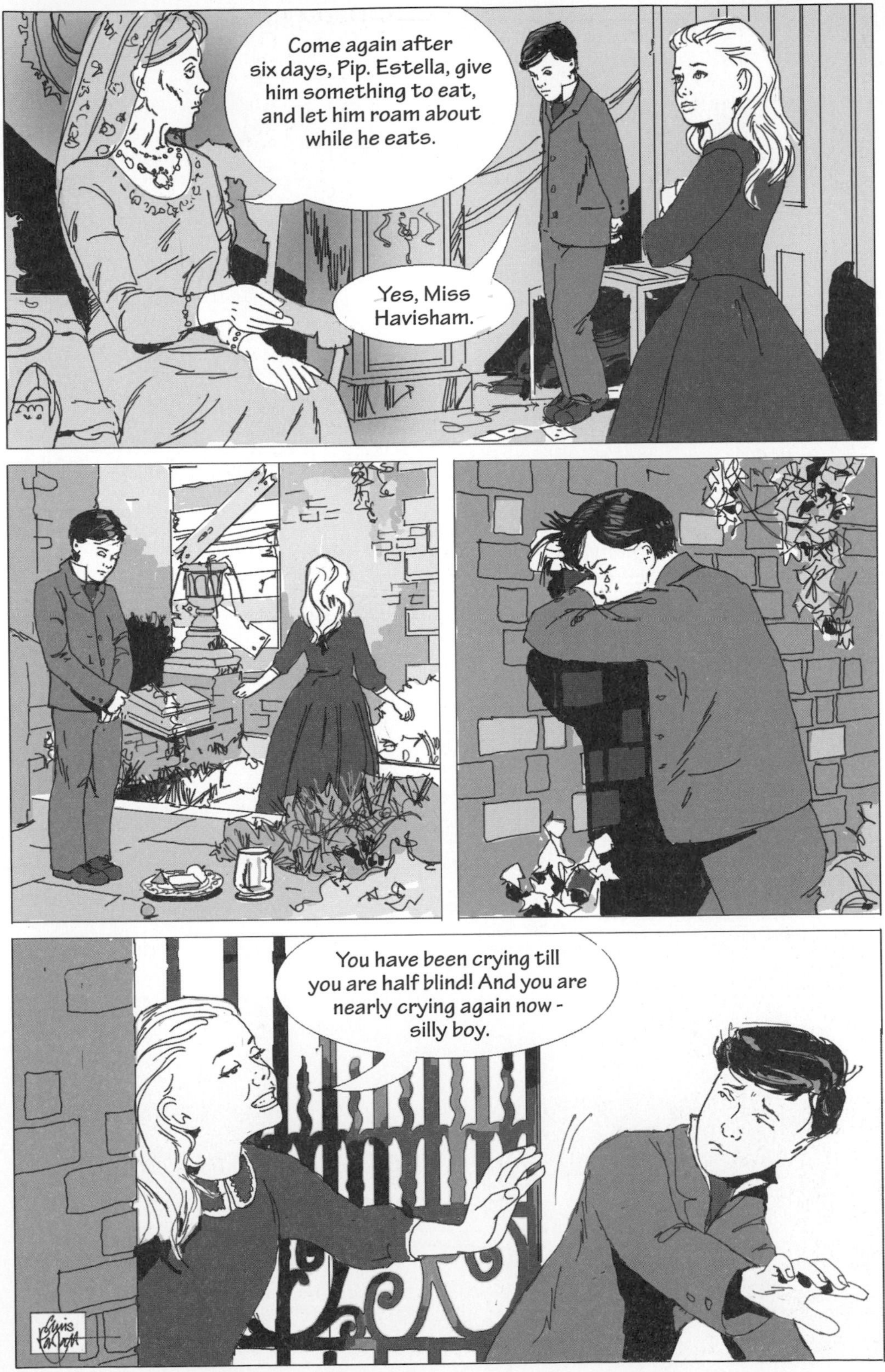
Come again after six days, Pip. Estella, give him something to eat, and let him roam about while he eats.
Yes, Miss Havisham.
You have been crying till you are half blind! And you are nearly crying again now - silly boy.

Well! How did you get on?

Er... pretty well, Uncle Pumblechook.

BACK AT HOME...

Speak up, boy! What is Miss Havisham like?

Er... very tall and dark.

She was sitting in a black velvet coach and Miss Estella - that's her niece, I think - handed her cake and wine on gold plates.

And we played with flags, and I saw swords and pistols and jam in a cupboard!

LATER...

Joe, all those things I said about Miss Havisham were lies. I just didn't want to talk about Miss Havisham and Estella. They said I was a common working boy.

But you told lies, Pip, and there's one thing you may be sure of - namely that lies is lies, and lies are wicked. Don't you tell no more of them, Pip.

I WANTED TO LEARN TO READ AND WRITE....

BUT WE DIDN'T LEARN MUCH.

Here's a likely young parcel of bones. What do you call him?

Pip.

ONE DAY AFTER SCHOOL I MET JOE AND A STRANGE MAN IN THE PUB...

He's stirring his drink with the file I gave to the convict in the churchyard!

There you are, it's yours! Your very own shilling.

Look, a man at the Three Jolly Bargemen gave me this!

What's this? Two one-pound notes? He must have made a mistake. He's sure to come back for them. I'll put them away.

I WENT TO MISS HAVISHAM'S EVERY WEEK.

Am I pretty, Pip?

Yes, I think you are very pretty, Estella.

Am I insulting?

Not so insulting as you were last time.

Now, you coarse little monster, what do you think of me now? Why don't you cry again, you little wretch?

Because, Estella, I'll never cry for you again!

How do you come here?

WE BUMPED INTO A MAN ON THE STAIRS.

Miss Havisham sent for me, sir.

Well! Behave yourself. I know a lot about little boys, and you're a bad set of fellows. Now mind! You behave yourself.

I ENTERED MISS HAVISHAM'S ROOM.

This is where I shall be laid when I am dead.

ESTELLA ENTERED WITH SOME MEMBERS OF MISS HAVISHAM'S FAMILY.

Dear Miss Havisham, how well you look!

Indeed I do not, Sarah Pocket. I am yellow skin and bones. Now go, all of you.

LATER, IN THE GARDEN...

Who let you in?

Miss Estella.

Come and fight me.

Come here, Pip! You may kiss me if you like.

I think she was watching our fight, and saw me win.

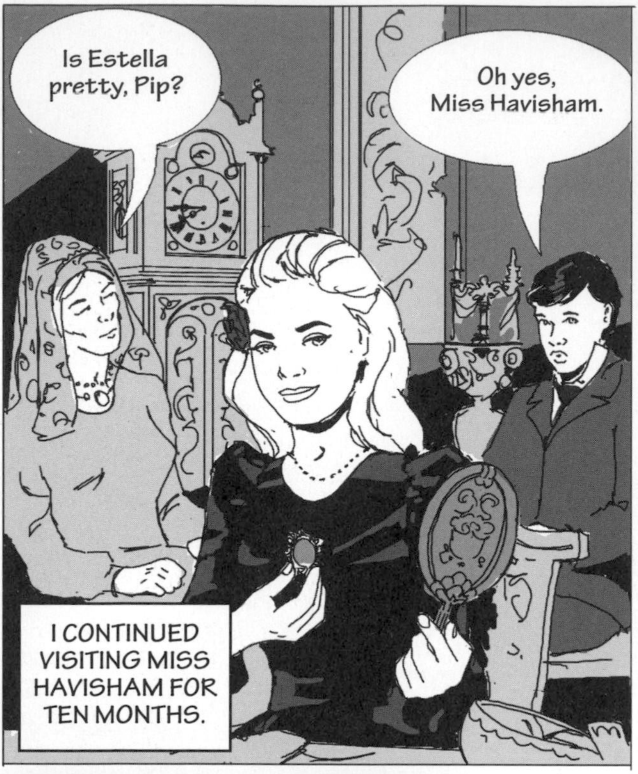
Is Estella pretty, Pip?
Oh yes, Miss Havisham.
I CONTINUED VISITING MISS HAVISHAM FOR TEN MONTHS.

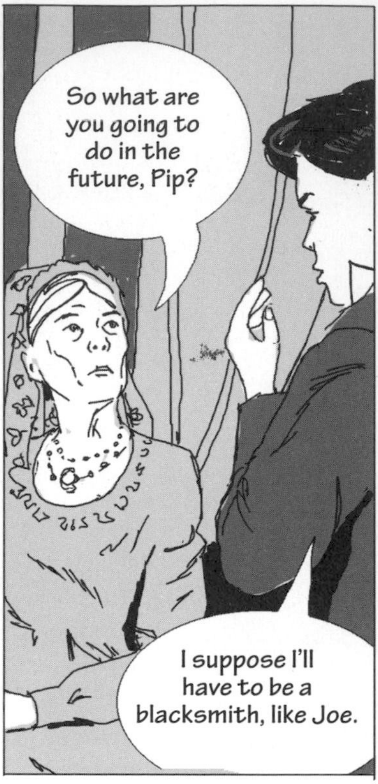
So what are you going to do in the future, Pip?
I suppose I'll have to be a blacksmith, like Joe.

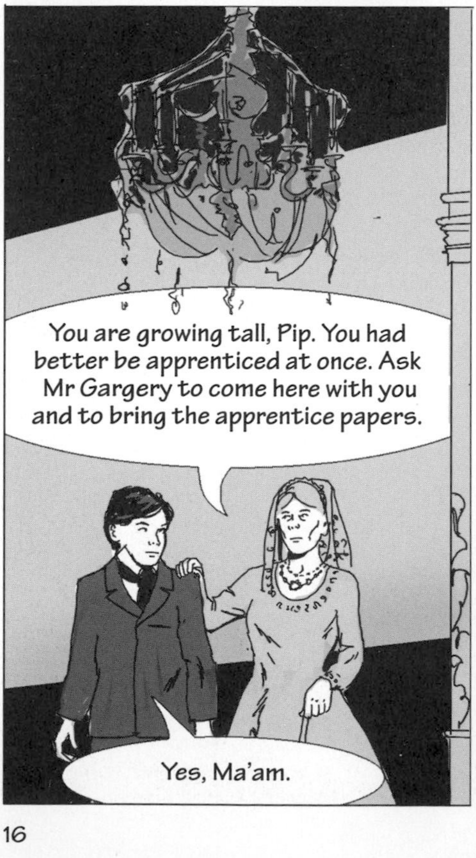
You are growing tall, Pip. You had better be apprenticed at once. Ask Mr Gargery to come here with you and to bring the apprentice papers.
Yes, Ma'am.

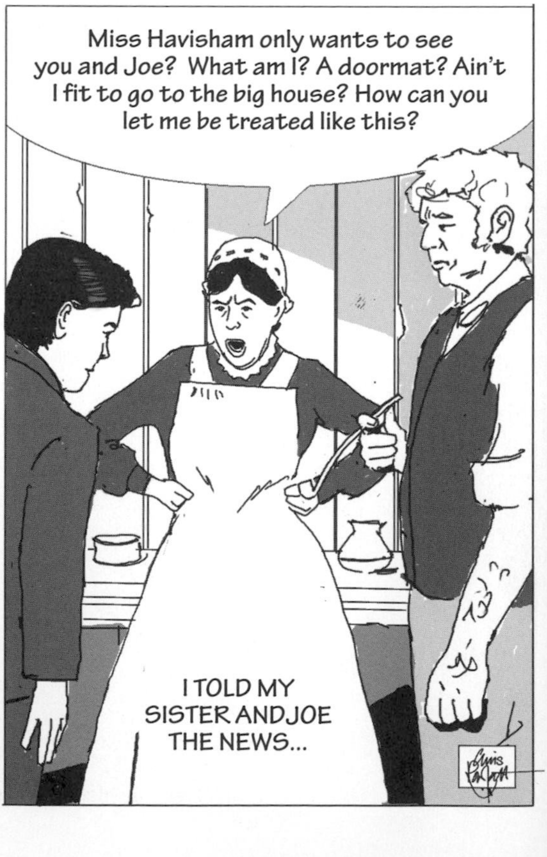
Miss Havisham only wants to see you and Joe? What am I? A doormat? Ain't I fit to go to the big house? How can you let me be treated like this?
I TOLD MY SISTER ANDJOE THE NEWS...

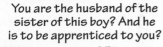

You are the husband of the sister of this boy? And he is to be apprenticed to you?

You know, Pip, you and me always were friends, and we have looked forward to it.

Has the boy ever made any objection? Does he like the trade?

You know Pip, it was the wish of your heart.

Have you brought the papers with you?

Here they are, Pip.

Pip has earned some money here, and here it is. There are five and twenty guineas in this bag. Give it to your master, Pip.

This is very generous of you, Pip. Thank you.

Am I to come again, Miss Havisham?

No, Gargery is your master now. Good-by, Pip. Let them out, Estella.

Pip earned it. It's five and twenty guineas.

I liked Joe's trade once, but that was before I met Estella.

I'm glad Estella can't see me now.

As we aren't busy in the forge just now, would you give me a half day tomorrow? I would like to call on Miss Est- Havisham.

Which her name ain't Est- Havisham, Pip. But yes, I suppose you could.

Is it all right if I go now, Joe?

If young Pip has a half day, what about me?

Well, Orlick, you work as well as most men. Let's all have a half day.

You fool, Joe Gargery! Giving half days to great idle hulkers like that Orlick, wasting wages!

I heard that, Mother Gargery. You're a foul shrew. If you was my wife I'd hold you under the pump and choke it out of you!

CUFF

Oh! To hear him! That Orlick! In my own house! With my husband standing by... Oh! Oh!

WHEN I LEFT THE FORGE TO GO TO MISS HAVISHAM'S, EVERYTHING SEEMED CALM AGAIN.

Mrs Joe, eh? On the Rampage, Pip, and off the Rampage, Pip - such is life!

You may leave us, Sarah Pocket. Hello, Pip. I hope you want nothing from me? You'll get nothing.

No, Miss Havisham. I only wanted you to know that I am doing well in my apprenticeship.

Ah, but you are really here to see Estella! Well, she's abroad - far out of reach, prettier than ever, admired by all who see her. Do you feel that you've lost her? Poor Pip....

19

THAT EVENING...

Halloa! Is that Orlick?

Ah! Mr Wopsle and Pip - I was waiting for company.

The guns is going again. More escaped convicts.

BANG BANG

There's something wrong up at your place, Pip. We must run.

She's been hit with that leg iron!

Mrs Joe is alive - just - but she will never go on the Rampage again...

This was filed off some time ago...

MRS JOE COULD NO LONGER LOOK AFTER HERSELF. BIDDY, A GIRL FROM THE VILLAGE, CAME TO HELP.

Biddy, you always seem to know what my sister wants, even though she can't speak.

She's good at drawing what she wants. That's a hammer.

Don't you see? She means him, Orlick!

Good day, Miss Havisham. You asked to see me on my birthday, so here I am.

Here's a guinea for you, Pip. Be sure to come on your next birthday.

I SPENT THE MONEY TO IMPROVE MY LEARNING.

Biddy, I want to be a gentleman. I don't want to be a blacksmith.

Don't you think you are happier as you are?

It's because of the beautiful young lady at Miss Havisham's: she's more beautiful than anybody. I want to be a gentleman for her, but she told me that I'm coarse and common.

That was neither very true nor very polite.

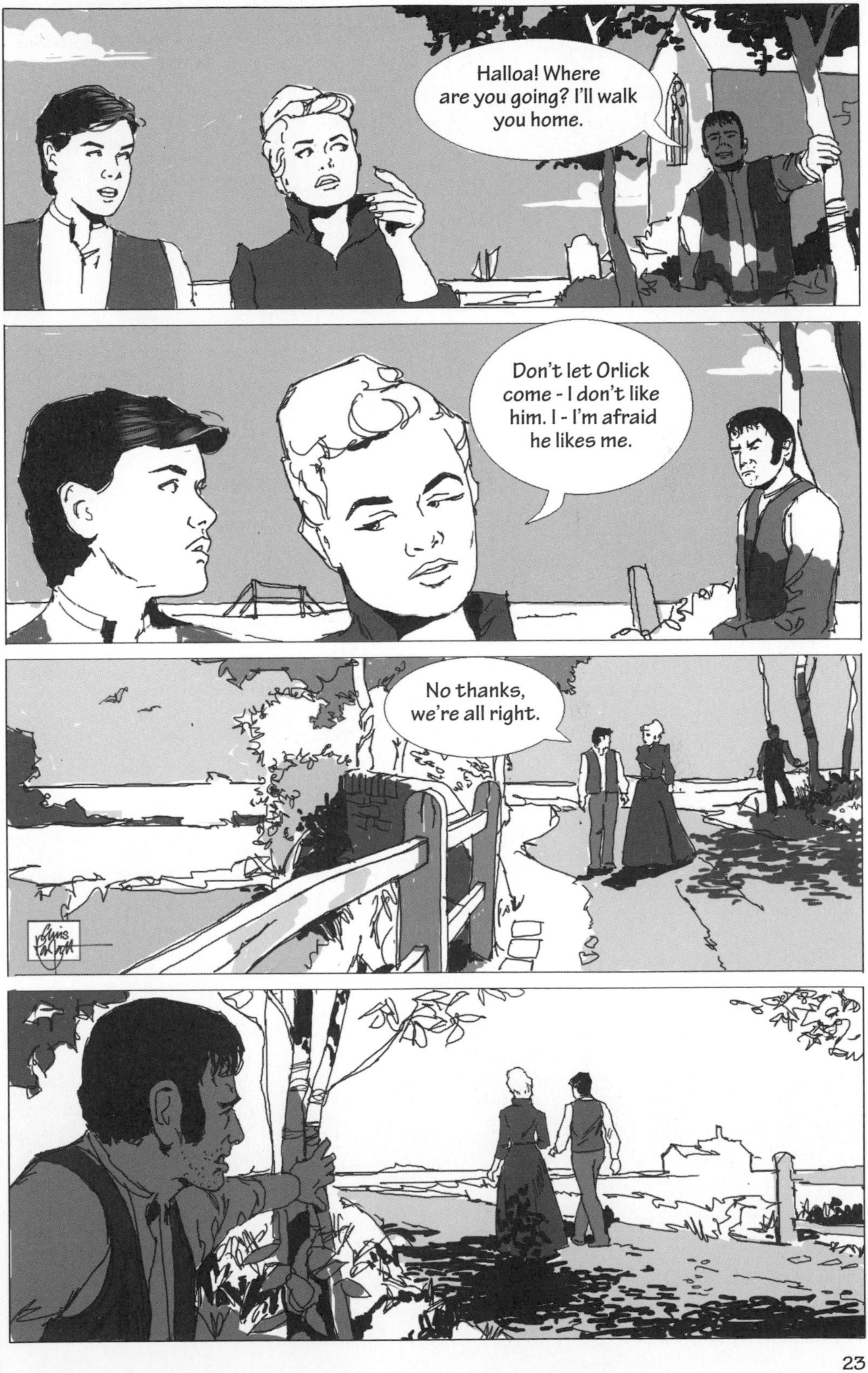
Halloa! Where are you going? I'll walk you home.
Don't let Orlick come - I don't like him. I - I'm afraid he likes me.
No thanks, we're all right.

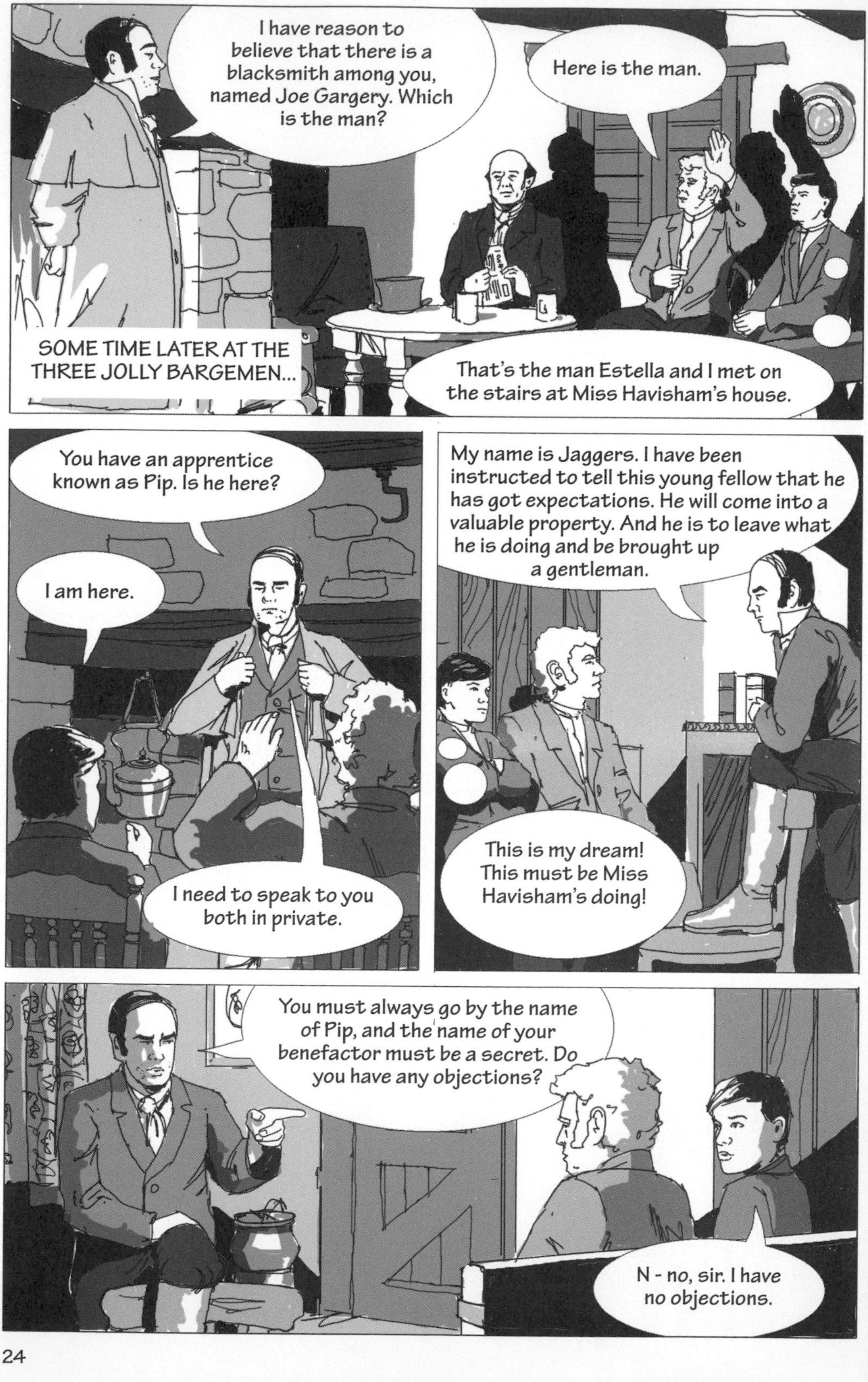
I have reason to believe that there is a blacksmith among you, named Joe Gargery. Which is the man?
Here is the man.
SOME TIME LATER AT THE THREE JOLLY BARGEMEN...
That's the man Estella and I met on the stairs at Miss Havisham's house.
You have an apprentice known as Pip. Is he here?
I am here.
I need to speak to you both in private.
My name is Jaggers. I have been instructed to tell this young fellow that he has got expectations. He will come into a valuable property. And he is to leave what he is doing and be brought up a gentleman.
This is my dream! This must be Miss Havisham's doing!
You must always go by the name of Pip, and the name of your benefactor must be a secret. Do you have any objections?
N - no, sir. I have no objections.

You are to have a good education, and I have the money to pay for it. You will need a proper tutor, and I have one in mind - Mr Matthew Pocket. You can meet his son, who is in London.

You'll need new clothes. I'll leave you twenty guineas. One week from today you will take the coach into London. I'll send you my address.

I am also to offer you, Joseph Gargery, a sum of money in compensation for the loss of Pip's services as your apprentice.

Pip is free to go, Mr Jaggers, but no money can compensate for the loss of the little lad that came to the forge - ever the best of friends, Pip.

So Pip's a gentleman of fortune, then, and God bless him in it.

God bless him!

It's a pity Joe has such rough ways, he won't fit into my new life at all...

Biddy, Joe is a dear, good fellow, but he is rather backward in his learning and his manners. I hope you'll help him on a little.

Help him on? Won't his manners do, then?

Mr Trabb, I have come into a handsome property. I need a fashionable suit to go to London.

Well, well, my dear sir. You have come to the right tailors! Will you do me the honour of stepping into the shop?

You must be hungry, you must be exhausted. Be seated, Pip. Here's chicken, and roast beef. Let us have a drink.

I am treated quite differently now I have money, even by Uncle Pumblechook!

I start for London tomorrow, Miss Havisham. I have come to say goodbye.

You are adopted by a rich person?

I PAID A FINAL VISIT TO MISS HAVISHAM.

I have come into such good fortune since I saw you last, Miss Havisham, and I am so grateful for it, Miss Havisham.

Yes, yes. I have seen Mr Jaggers. I have heard about it. You have a promising career ahead of you. Be good, and follow Mr Jaggers' instructions.

Goodbye, Pip. You will always keep the name of Pip, you know.

Yes, Miss Havisham.

A special meal for your last evening, Pip, to wish you good luck in London.

Good luck, Pip, old chap.

Hooroar!

WHEN I GOT TO LONDON, I WENT STRAIGHT TO MR JAGGERS' OFFICE.

Mr. Jaggers
Attorney at Law

Is Mr Jaggers in?

He's at court at present. He asked that you wait. My name is Wemmick.

FINALLY, MR JAGGERS ARRIVED.

Wemmick, my clerk, will take you round to Barnard's Inn to young Mr Pocket's rooms. Later you'll go to his father's house - see how you like it there.

You'll have an allowance for your expenses - anything within reason.

TO LET

TO LET

BARNARD'S INN WAS RATHER SHABBY.

MR. POCKET, Junior

Return Shortly

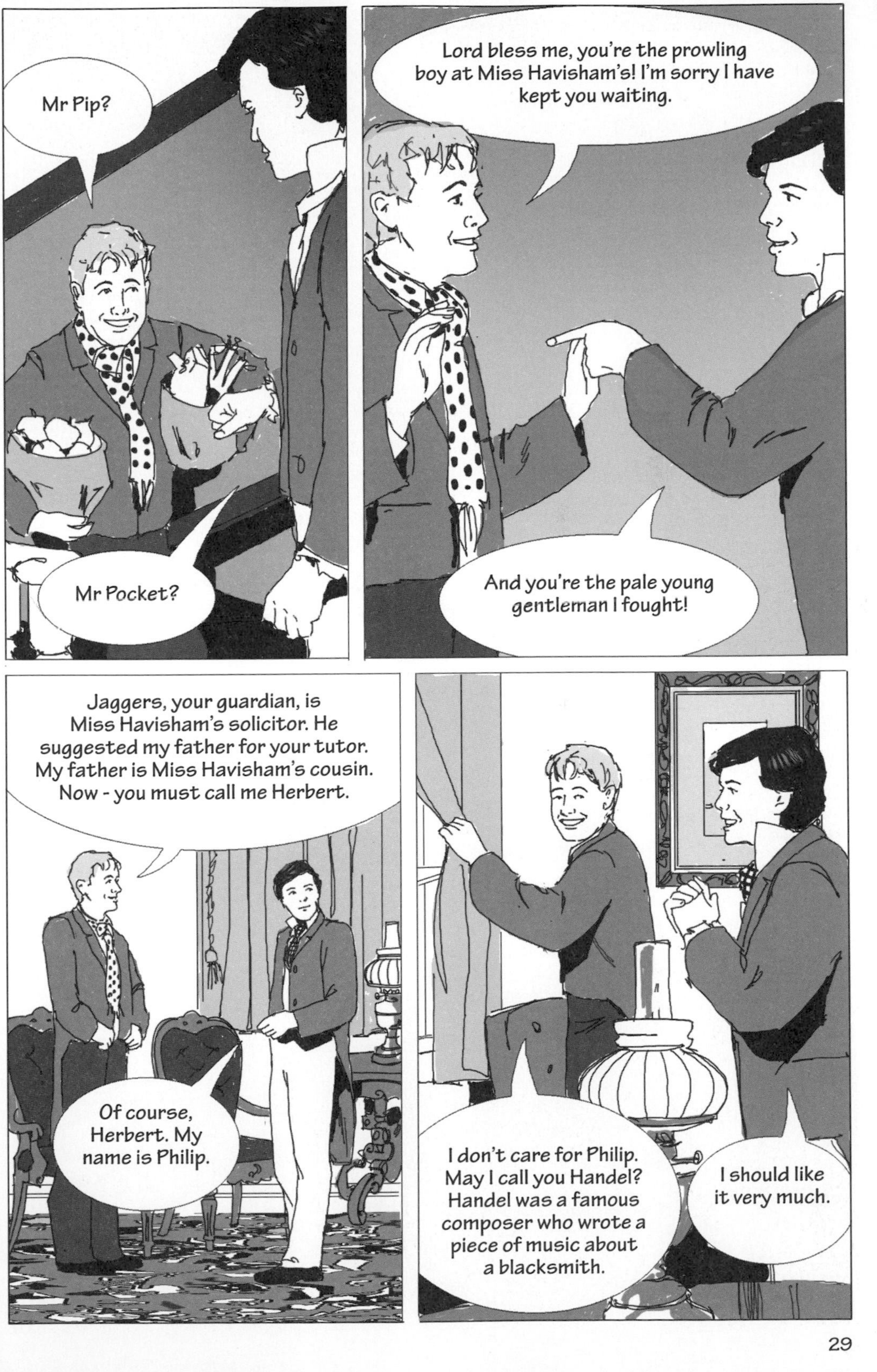
Mr Pip?
Mr Pocket?
Lord bless me, you're the prowling boy at Miss Havisham's! I'm sorry I have kept you waiting.
And you're the pale young gentleman I fought!
Jaggers, your guardian, is Miss Havisham's solicitor. He suggested my father for your tutor. My father is Miss Havisham's cousin. Now - you must call me Herbert.
Of course, Herbert. My name is Philip.
I don't care for Philip. May I call you Handel? Handel was a famous composer who wrote a piece of music about a blacksmith.
I should like it very much.

Tell me about Miss Havisham. Why is she so strange?

As a child, Miss Havisham was very spoilt. Her father was rich, and gave her everything she wanted.

When Miss Havisham's mother died, her father married again. He had another child, Miss Havisham's half-brother. He was bad - wasteful, disobedient, and always drunk.

After their father died, he introduced her to an evil but charming man. She fell in love, and they planned to marry.

The marriage day was fixed, the wedding clothes were bought, the wedding guests were invited. The day came but not the bridegroom. She received a letter...

At twenty minutes to nine?

That was the hour and minute at which she stopped all the clocks in the house.

Later it was learnt that her fiancé was a swindler. He and her half-brother cheated her out of a lot of money.

No one knows where they are now.

And that, Handel, is why Miss Havisham has brought up Estella to be selfish and proud, and to get revenge on all the male sex.

What relation is she to Miss Havisham?

No relation at all. She's adopted.

HERBERT AND I GOT ON VERY WELL.

This is where I work, Handel. I don't get paid, but I reckon that sooner or later it will lead to a good business opportunity.

Mamma, this is young Pip.

HERBERT TOOK ME HOME TO MEET HIS FAMILY.

MR AND MRS POCKET HAD A LOT OF CHILDREN!

Millers, would you bring the baby? I hear crying.

Belinda, I hope you have welcomed Mr Pip?

Yes.

I MET MR POCKET...

This is your room, Pip.

And these are your fellow guests - Mr Drummle and Mr Startop.

You naughty child, how dare you take away Baby's toy? Go and sit down!

But Mama dear, Baby could put his eyes out!

Belinda, Jane is only trying to help.

I will not allow anyone to interfere. I'm surprised at you, Matthew.

Good God! Are infants to poke their eyes out and nobody save them?

This is great fun! I think I'll get myself a boat.

I WENT TO SEE MR JAGGERS...

...And so, Mr Jaggers, I know I can learn a lot from staying with Mr Matthew Pocket, but I'd like to keep my room at Barnard's Inn, too.

Good! I told you you'd get on with young Herbert. How much money will you need?

Suppose you make it twenty pounds?

Wemmick! Pay Mr Pip twenty pounds.

Welcome to my home, Pip. I did it all myself. Do come and meet the Aged Parent.

WEMMICK INVITED ME TO SEE HIS AMAZING HOUSE.

Aged Parent, how are you? Here's Mr Pip.

THIS IS A FINE PLACE OF MY SON'S, SIR!

I hope Mr Jaggers admires this place of yours, Wemmick?

He's never heard of it. No, the office is one thing and private life is another. I've never spoken about it.

JAGGERS INVITED HERBERT, DRUMMLE, STARTOP AND MYSELF TO DINNER.

Pip, who's the blotchy, sprawly, sulky fellow over there?

That's Bentley Drummle, Mr Jaggers. The one with the delicate face is Startop.

She looks familiar!

Look at that muscle, Mr Jaggers!

I'll show you a wrist, Drummle. Where's my housekeeper? Molly, let them see both of your wrists.

There's power here. Very few men have the power of wrist that this woman has. That'll do, Molly. You can go.

Gentlemen, I am sorry to announce that it's half-past nine. We must break up.

Goodbye, Pip. I like that Drummle.

I am glad you like him, sir, but I don't.

34

BACK IN MY ROOMS, I HAD HIRED A SERVANT NAMED PEPPER.

A letter from Biddy. Joe is coming to see me at nine o'clock on Tuesday. Pepper, you be here at eight that morning to make sure everything is ready.

Mr Gargery.

How are you, Joe?

How AIR you, Pip?

How do you do, Mr Gargery? I'm Herbert Pocket. When did you come to town?

Yesterday afternoon? No, it were not. Yes, it were... Yes. It were yesterday afternoon.

Pip, I've got a message for you. Miss Havisham told Pumblechook to tell you that Estella has come home and would be glad to see you.

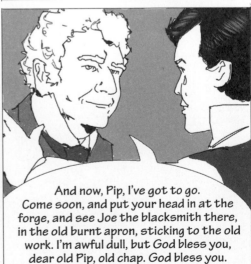

And now, Pip, I've got to go. Come soon, and put your head in at the forge, and see Joe the blacksmith there, in the old burnt apron, sticking to the old work. I'm awful dull, but God bless you, dear old Pip, old chap. God bless you.

Goodbye, Handel.

Up there on top - that's the man with the file from the Three Jolly Bargemen.

I SET OFF BACK TO THE VILLAGE TO SEE ESTELLA.

I SAT ON TOP OF THE COACH. BEHIND ME WERE TWO CONVICTS WITH THEIR JAILER.

Two one-pound notes?

Two one-pound notes!

Yes, he gave them to me when I got out of prison. He says, would I find that boy that fed him and kept his secret, and give him the two one-pound notes? I said I would, and I did.

So that money came from an escaped convict!

I SHOULD HAVE STAYED WITH JOE AT THE FORGE, BUT WENT TO THE INN INSTEAD.

Blue Boar Inn

Orlick! Have you left the forge?

AT MISS HAVISHAM'S I GOT A SURPRISE.

Do this look like a forge?

This is my room, the porter's room. It's like a cage for a human dormouse.

Come in, Pip. How do you do? So you kiss my hand as if I were a queen, eh?

I heard that you were so kind as to wish me to come and see you, and I came directly.

Do you find her much changed, Pip? Estella was proud and insulting, and you wanted to get away from her. Remember?

Er... I didn't know any better, Miss Havisham.

Well, is Pip changed, Estella?

Very much.

Is he less coarse and common, perhaps?

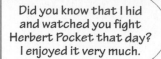

Did you know that I hid and watched you fight Herbert Pocket that day? I enjoyed it very much.

You gave me a nice reward. You let me kiss you. Herbert and I are great friends now.

I must tell you, Pip, I have no heart - no softness, no sympathy or sentiment.

She reminds me of someone, but who?

Let's go in.

I am sure Miss Havisham has chosen us for one another.

Is Estella beautiful and graceful? Do you admire her?

Everyone must who sees her, Miss Havisham.

Love her, love her, love her! If she tears your heart to pieces, love her!

LATER, JAGGERS JOINED US FOR CARDS.

I THOUGHT OF ESTELLA THAT NIGHT...

Love her!

Love her!

LOVE HER!

Mr Jaggers, I don't think that Orlick should be working for Miss Havisham. He has a bad temper and we think that he may have tried to kill my sister.

Very good, Pip. I'll go round and pay him off. Send him on his way. He won't argue with me.

AT THE BLUE BOAR, OVER BREAKFAST...

My dear Herbert, I have something to tell you. I love - I adore - Estella!

Of course, I know that!

BACK IN LONDON...

But Pip, think of what Miss Havisham has tried to make her. Think of what Estella is herself. She could make you very miserable, Pip.

I know it, Herbert, but I can't help it.

I haven't told you, Pip, that I myself am engaged to be married - to a young lady named Clara. But you can't marry, you know, when you have no money and no future.

I should very much like to meet the young lady.

You shall.

I say, Herbert, look at this! My friend Mr Wopsle is playing Hamlet at the theatre.

To be, or not to be, that is the question. Whether 'tis nobler in the mind to suffer the slings and arrows of outrageous fortune, or...

Yes!

No!

Ha, ha!

Toss for it!

Gentlemen, how good of you to come! What did you think of the play?

Excellent!

Very good indeed.

Ah yes, indeed. The play's the thing!

AT LAST, ESTELLA CAME TO LONDON.

Would you like to rest?

Yes, I am to rest a little, and I am to drink some tea, and you are to take care of me all the while.

So - where will you be staying in London?

I am to live at Richmond with a lady who will be taking me about and introducing me.

And how do you get on with Mr Pocket and his family?

I live quite pleasantly there - as pleasantly as I could live anywhere away from you.

You silly boy, how can you talk such nonsense?

I STOOD LOOKING AT THE HOUSE WHERE SHE WAS TO STAY, THINKING HOW HAPPY I SHOULD BE IF I LIVED THERE WITH HER, AND KNOWING THAT I WAS NEVER HAPPY WITH HER, BUT MISERABLE.

41

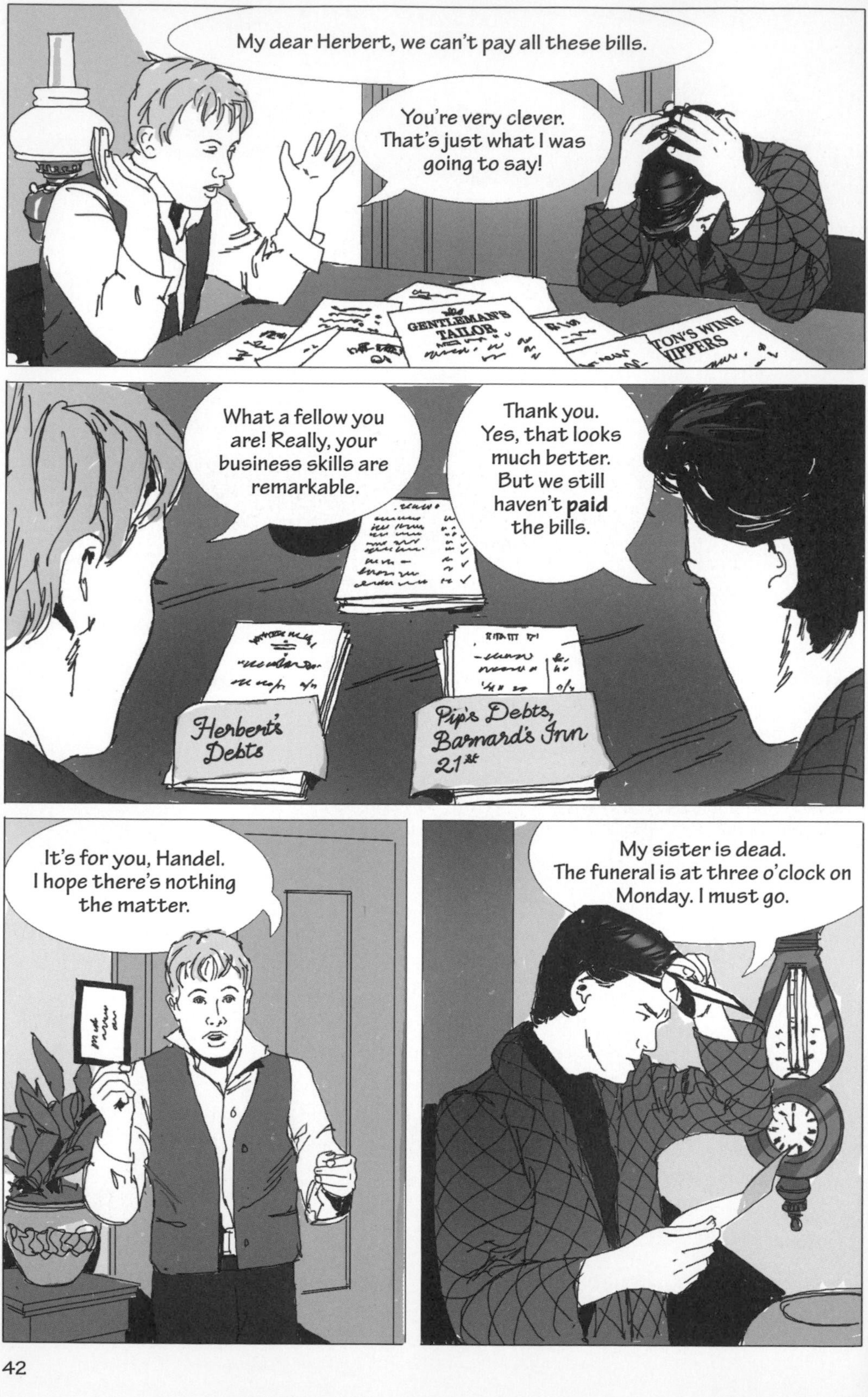

My dear Herbert, we can't pay all these bills.
You're very clever. That's just what I was going to say!
GENTLEMAN'S TAILOR
What a fellow you are! Really, your business skills are remarkable.
Thank you. Yes, that looks much better. But we still haven't **paid** the bills.
Herbert's Debts
Pip's Debts, Barnard's Inn 21st
It's for you, Handel. I hope there's nothing the matter.
My sister is dead. The funeral is at three o'clock on Monday. I must go.

Do you know what became of Orlick, Biddy?

I saw him on the night she died. And I saw him over there a minute ago - now he is gone.

Goodbye, dear Joe. I shall be down again soon, and often.

Never too soon, and never too often, Pip.

BACK IN LONDON I SAW JAGGERS.

Pip! You are twenty-one years old today. I must call you Mr Pip now. Congratulations.

Thank you, sir.

Now read this.

This is a bank note for five hundred pounds!

That money is yours, and you will receive the same amount every year. And your benefactor wishes to meet you.

Will that be soon, Mr Jaggers?

That is a question you must not ask. When you meet your benefactor my part in this business will end.

Miss Havisham must be my benefactor. Obviously she has not told him her plans for Estella and me.

I PAID A VISIT TO WEMMICK'S HOUSE.

I need your advice, Wemmick. I'm worried about Herbert's future. Can you suggest some way I could help him?

Mr Pip, that is very good of you. I'll give it some thought.

Mr Pip, this is Miss Skiffins, my ladyfriend. Her brother may be able to help us.

LATER...

With the help of your money, we have found a small partnership for Herbert. It should suit him very well.

Remember, he must never know about my help in this matter.

HERBERT HEARD THE NEWS.

Such wonderful news, Handel. I have been offered a place at last! I can hardly believe it!

Well done, Herbert. Well done! I am very happy for you.

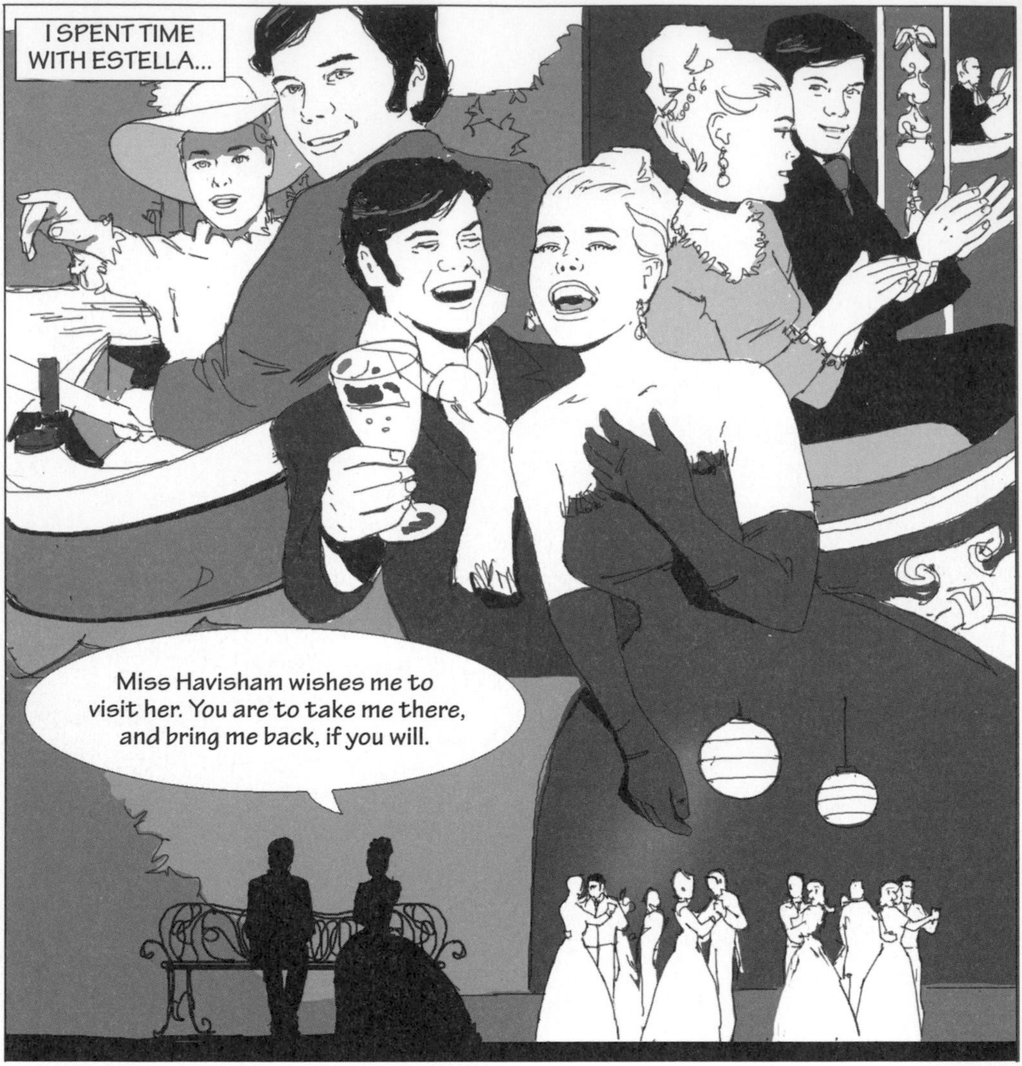
I SPENT TIME WITH ESTELLA...
Miss Havisham wishes me to visit her. You are to take me there, and bring me back, if you will.

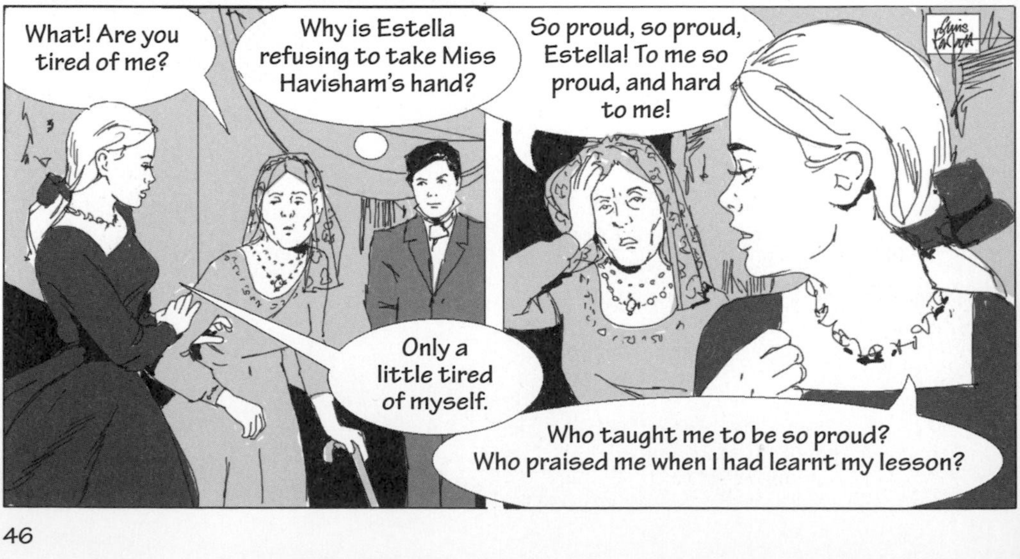
What! Are you tired of me?
Why is Estella refusing to take Miss Havisham's hand?
Only a little tired of myself.
So proud, so proud, Estella! To me so proud, and hard to me!
Who taught me to be so proud? Who praised me when I had learnt my lesson?

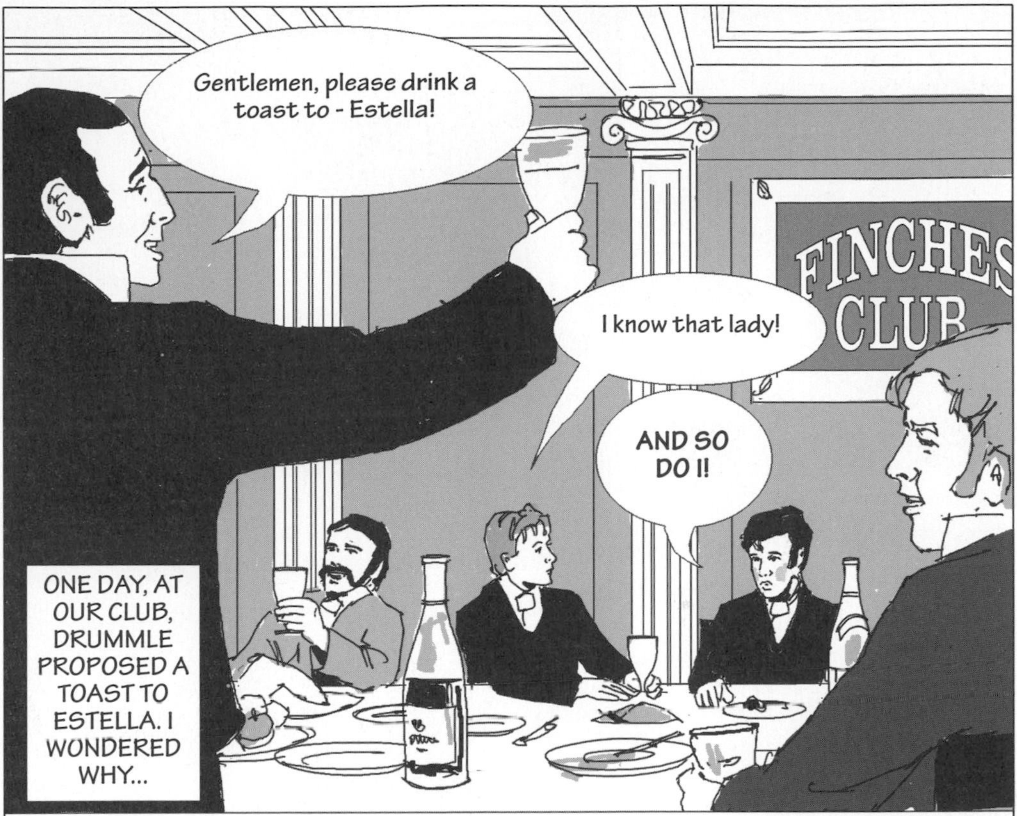
ONE DAY, AT OUR CLUB, DRUMMLE PROPOSED A TOAST TO ESTELLA. I WONDERED WHY...
Gentlemen, please drink a toast to - Estella!
I know that lady!
AND SO DO I!
FINCHES CLUB

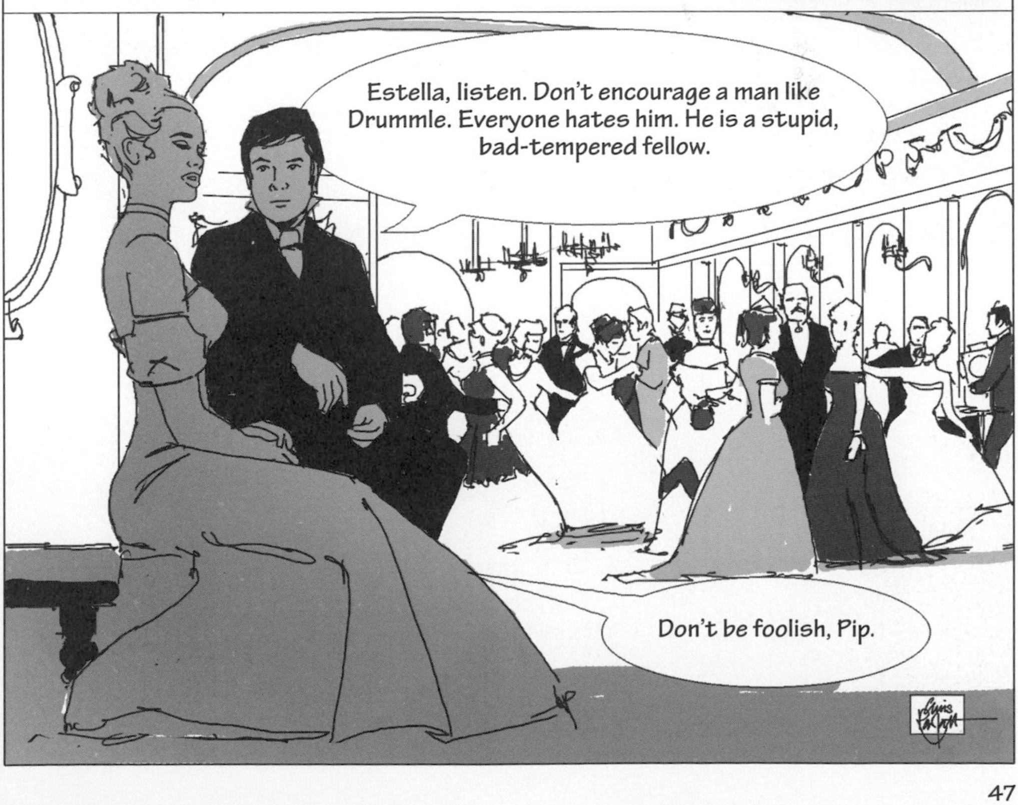
Estella, listen. Don't encourage a man like Drummle. Everyone hates him. He is a stupid, bad-tempered fellow.
Don't be foolish, Pip.

There's someone down there - what floor do you want?

Top floor - Mr Pip.

Do you wish to come in?

Yes, I wish to come in, Master.

You acted noble in the marshes, my boy! And I have never forgot it.

The convict!

You are wet and tired, but you can't stay here, I have come into property now. But will you drink something before you go?

Might I ask whose property? And your income each year - it begins with five? You have a guardian whose name begins with J?

Yes, Pip, dear boy, it's me! I've made a gentleman of you! It's me what done it. I'm your second father. You're my son - more to me than any son. I've worked hard to earn money - for you to spend.

Where will you put me? I must be put somewhere, dear boy. I have to be careful - I was sent away for life. If I'm caught, it's death. I'll be hanged.

My friend is away for a few days. You may have his room.

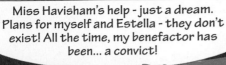
Miss Havisham's help - just a dream. Plans for myself and Estella - they don't exist! All the time, my benefactor has been... a convict!

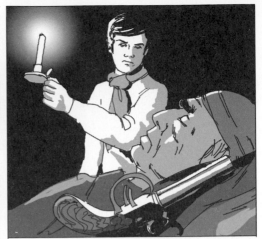

I shall tell everyone that you are my uncle - but I don't even know your name.

That's it, dear boy! Call me Uncle. And I'll use the name of Provis. But my real name is Magwitch. Abel Magwitch.

There's plenty of money in there, dear boy. There's more where that came from. It'll be my pleasure to see you spend it.

And how long will you stay here?

How long? I'm not going back - I've come for good.

49

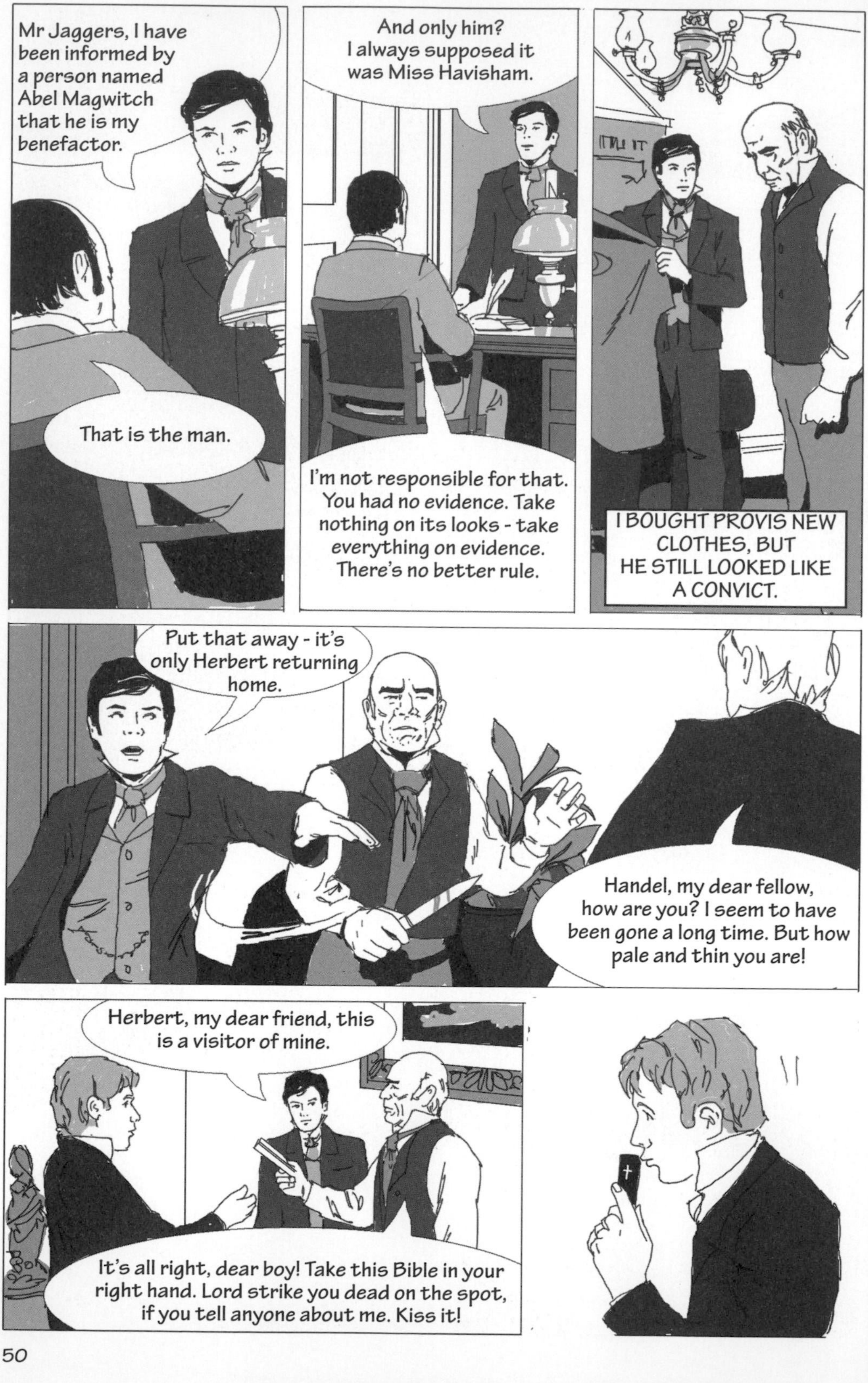
Mr Jaggers, I have been informed by a person named Abel Magwitch that he is my benefactor.
That is the man.
And only him? I always supposed it was Miss Havisham.
I'm not responsible for that. You had no evidence. Take nothing on its looks - take everything on evidence. There's no better rule.
I BOUGHT PROVIS NEW CLOTHES, BUT HE STILL LOOKED LIKE A CONVICT.
Put that away - it's only Herbert returning home.
Handel, my dear fellow, how are you? I seem to have been gone a long time. But how pale and thin you are!
Herbert, my dear friend, this is a visitor of mine.
It's all right, dear boy! Take this Bible in your right hand. Lord strike you dead on the spot, if you tell anyone about me. Kiss it!

This is the room I found for you, Provis. I hope you'll be comfortable here. Sleep well.

Thank'ee Pip. I'll see you tomorrow.

What is to be done?

My poor dear Handel. I am too shocked to think.

Remember when you were found on the marshes, fighting with another convict? Will you tell us about yourself and that other man?

The first and the main thing is to get him out of England. And you will have to go with him. Having found you, he won't go without you.

I'll give it to you short and handy: in jail and out of jail, in jail and out of jail. There, you've got it.

Tramping, thieving, begging, working sometimes. Then I met a man called Compeyson. He was a smooth talker, and good looking, too.

Compeyson had a friend called Arthur. Him and Compeyson had swindled a rich lady and made a pot of money. Arthur had terrible nightmares about the things they'd done. In the end, he died.

I can't get rid of her - all in white, with flowers in her hair. Aargh!

Compeyson swindled and stole. I helped him, but I was always the one who got caught. I was always the one who went to prison. He got off because he was posh.

In the end, Compeyson and I were both sent to prison. His sentence was seven years, but because of his lies, I got fourteen years. I told him I'd smash his face in, and I did.

For petty theft, two years. Take him away!

HERBERT WROTE ME A NOTE.

Miss Havisham's brother was named Arthur. Compeyson was the man she was supposed to marry...

If I'm going abroad with Provis, I must see Miss Havisham first.

I'll keep an eye on Provis while you're away.

I TOOK THE COACH TO THE BLUE BOAR...

Bentley Drummle! What's he doing here at the Blue Boar?

Have you been here long, Drummle?

Long enough to be tired of it. Waiter, is my horse ready?

It's at the door, sir.

By the way, the lady won't be riding today - it's raining. And I shan't be dining here this evening, I'm going to dine at the lady's.

Estella! He's here to see Estella!

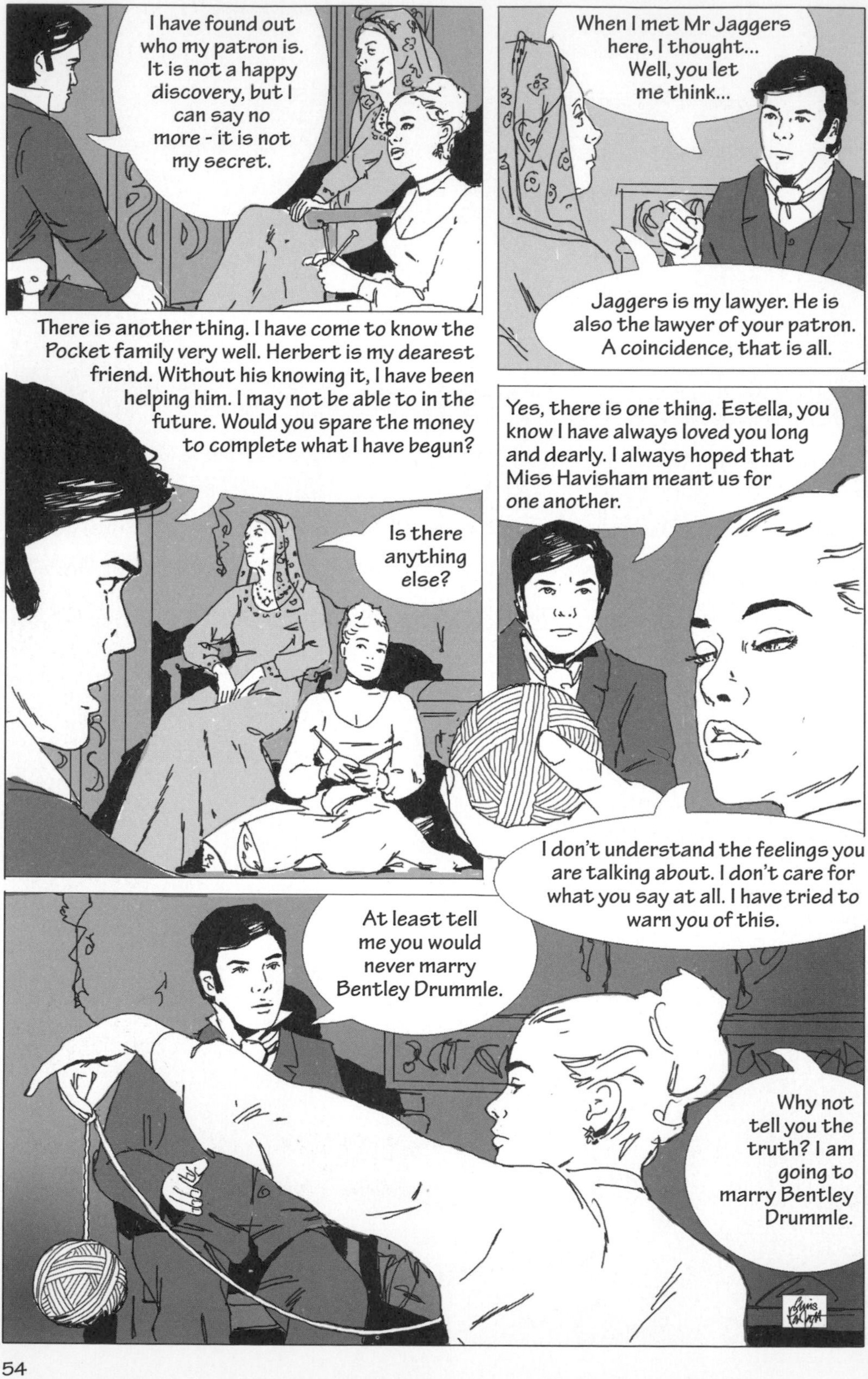
I have found out who my patron is. It is not a happy discovery, but I can say no more - it is not my secret.
When I met Mr Jaggers here, I thought... Well, you let me think...
Jaggers is my lawyer. He is also the lawyer of your patron. A coincidence, that is all.
There is another thing. I have come to know the Pocket family very well. Herbert is my dearest friend. Without his knowing it, I have been helping him. I may not be able to in the future. Would you spare the money to complete what I have begun?
Is there anything else?
Yes, there is one thing. Estella, you know I have always loved you long and dearly. I always hoped that Miss Havisham meant us for one another.
I don't understand the feelings you are talking about. I don't care for what you say at all. I have tried to warn you of this.
At least tell me you would never marry Bentley Drummle.
Why not tell you the truth? I am going to marry Bentley Drummle.

Good evening, Mr Pip, sir. I have a note for you.

PLEASE READ THIS HERE
Philip Pip Esquire

AT THE ENTRANCE TO MY LODGINGS IN LONDON...

Don't go home

This is Wemmick's writing. I must go to see him straightaway.

What is going on, Wemmick?

While you were away, we found that your rooms were being watched. Herbert got your friend to a safer place - a house on the river, near Greenwich.

Have you heard of a bad character, named Compeyson?

I have.

Is he alive?

He is.

Is he in London?

YES!

I WENT TO SEE PROVIS...

All is well, Handel. He's eager to see you. My fiancée Clara and her father live upstairs. Our friend is on the top floor.

BANG GRRRRRR BANG CRASH

That's her father. He drinks too much.

Handel, this is Clara.

I must go. Papa wants me, darling.

I hope you're comfortable here. Herbert did well, moving you so quickly. You'll be safer away from London.

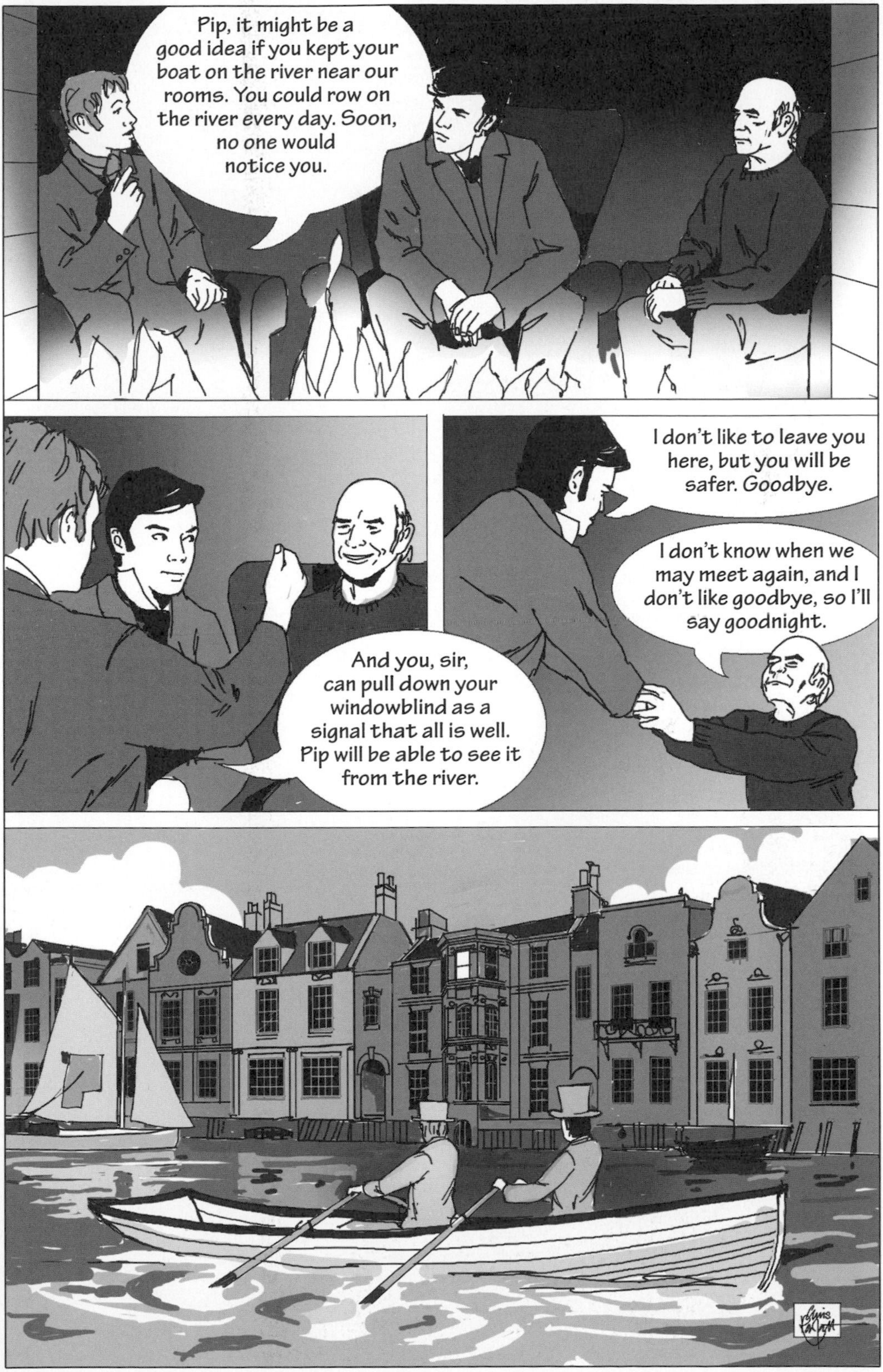
Pip, it might be a good idea if you kept your boat on the river near our rooms. You could row on the river every day. Soon, no one would notice you.
And you, sir, can pull down your windowblind as a signal that all is well. Pip will be able to see it from the river.
I don't like to leave you here, but you will be safer. Goodbye.
I don't know when we may meet again, and I don't like goodbye, so I'll say goodnight.

ONE NIGHT, I WENT TO SEE MR WOPSLE AT THE THEATRE AGAIN.

My dear Mr Wopsle, you saw me in the audience?

Yes I did. And guess what? Do you remember those two escaped convicts that were fighting in a ditch on the marshes, that Christmas long ago? Well, one of those prisoners was sitting behind you tonight. I saw him over your shoulder!

Which one was it?

The injured one. The one with cuts on his face.

COMPEYSON!

AT DINNER WITH JAGGERS AND WEMMICK...

Pip, here's a note from Miss Havisham. She wants to see you on a matter of business. You'll go?

Certainly I'll go. At once, I think.

Perhaps she has decided to help Herbert as I asked.

So, Pip! Our friend Bentley Drummle has won. He has married Estella. He may beat her up a bit, he's a violent man.

Surely you don't think he's scoundrel enough for that?

I didn't say so, Pip, but a fellow like him either beats or cringes. Here's to Mrs Bentley Drummle - what's the matter with you?

This subject is very painful to me.

I'm absolutely certain that this woman is Estella's mother. Her hands are Estella's hands. Her eyes are Estella's eyes. I'm sure of it.

Jaggers' housekeeper: Would you tell me about her, Wemmick? I have a reason for wanting to know.

Twenty or more years ago, that woman was accused of murder. Jaggers got her off. She worked for him ever since. At the time, she had a child about three years old. I don't know what happened to it.

Was the child a girl or a boy?

It was said to have been a girl.

Mr Jaggers gave me your note yesterday and I came straight away.

Thank you, thank you.

You said that you could tell me how to do something useful and good. Something you would like done.

Something that I would like done very much.

I have been secretly buying Herbert a partnership in a good firm, Clarrikers, but now it is not certain that I will be able to complete the purchase. It will cost nine hundred pounds.

This is a note to Jaggers, asking him to pay you the money.

And please, Pip, forgive me for all the pain I've caused you.

Oh, I can't bear to think about what I have done.

If you mean Estella, I should have loved her under any circumstances.

May I ask you about Estella?

Go on.

How did she come here?

Jaggers brought her.

Who is her mother?

I don't know.

I WALKED IN THE GARDEN, THINKING.

60

I'm leaving now, Miss Havisham.

Aaagh!

What have I done? What have I done? Forgive me...

HERBERT DRESSED MY BANDAGES.

These are nasty burns, Handel.

I sat with Provis last night, Handel - a good two hours. He told me a bit more about himself.

He said he was in love once. He and the woman had a child, a girl. When the child was about three, the woman was accused of murder. Jaggers was her lawyer. He got her off, but after the trial she and his daughter disappeared.

Did he tell you when this happened?

He said about twenty years ago. When you helped him in the graveyard, you were the same age that his daughter would have been.

I say, dear boy, you are rather excited. Are you quite yourself?

Yes, I am quite myself. But listen, Herbert. THE MAN YOU HAVE BEEN HIDING DOWN THE RIVER IS ESTELLA'S FATHER!

62

Though I did my best to save her, Miss Havisham's life hangs by a thread, Mr Jaggers.

Before the accident she told me all that she knew about Estella, her adopted daughter. And we know more. We know who the mother is, don't we, Mr Jaggers? She's your housekeeper.

Perhaps I know more of Estella's history than even you. I know her father too.

So you know the young lady's father, Pip?

Yes, his name is Provis - the convict. But he has no idea that his daughter is alive.

So, does this secret leave this room? Think! Estella would be disgraced if the secret of her parents became known. The disgrace would last all her life.

Do we agree to keep this story quiet?

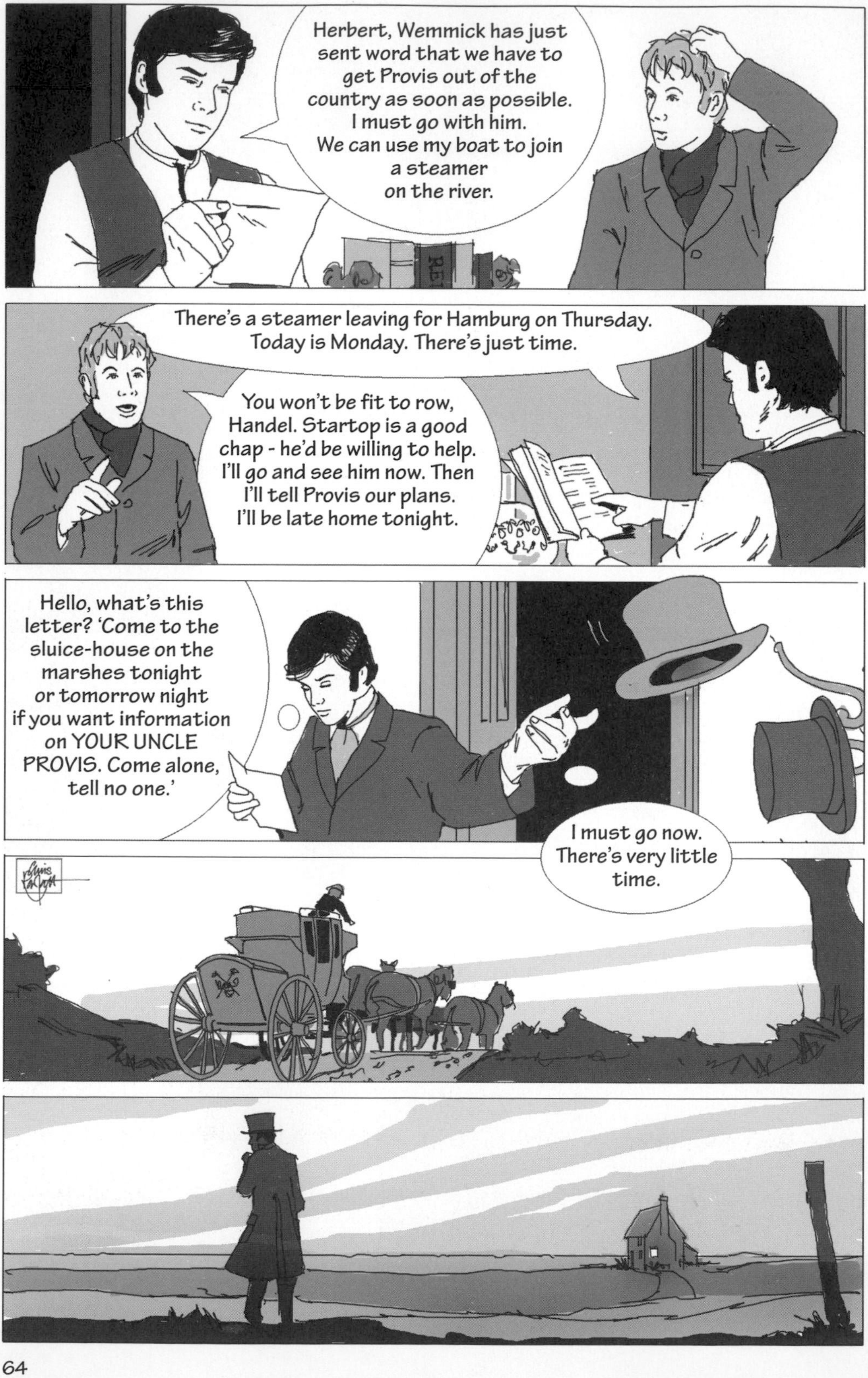
Herbert, Wemmick has just sent word that we have to get Provis out of the country as soon as possible. I must go with him. We can use my boat to join a steamer on the river.
There's a steamer leaving for Hamburg on Thursday. Today is Monday. There's just time.
You won't be fit to row, Handel. Startop is a good chap - he'd be willing to help. I'll go and see him now. Then I'll tell Provis our plans. I'll be late home tonight.
Hello, what's this letter? 'Come to the sluice-house on the marshes tonight or tomorrow night if you want information on YOUR UNCLE PROVIS. Come alone, tell no one.'
I must go now. There's very little time.

Now, I've got you!

Orlick! Let me go! Let me go!

It was me as did for your sister. You was favoured and Orlick was bullied and beaten. It was your fault. I giv' it 'er. I come upon 'er from behind, like tonight. I left 'er for dead.

I've followed you everywhere - I know all about Provis, yes I do, and Compeyson. Now I'm going to have yer life.

SUDDENLY, THE DOOR FLEW OPEN...

How did you know where I was, Herbert? How did you find me?

In your hurry to leave, you dropped Orlick's note on the floor. Startop and I followed you. Trabb's boy showed us the way to the sluice-house. Now get some rest, we leave tomorrow.

THE NEXT DAY...

WE PICKED UP PROVIS.

We'll spend the night here and wait for the steamer.

THE NEXT DAY WE SET OFF TO MEET THE STEAMER. AS WE DREW CLOSE...

AHOY! You have a convict there - Abel Magwitch, otherwise known as Provis. Hand him over!

Look out! That's Compeyson!

BOTH COMPEYSON AND PROVIS WENT OVERBOARD. COMPEYSON FELL UNDER THE THRASHING PADDLES OF THE STEAMER.

HALF DROWNED, PROVIS WAS PULLED OUT OF THE WATER. COMPEYSON WAS NEVER SEEN AGAIN.

I will never move from your side, so long as I am allowed to be near you. I will be as true to you, as you have been to me.

My dear Handel, I shall have to leave you. The firm is sending me to Cairo. Perhaps you could join me there?

For now, I want to be with Magwitch, for we must call him that now, until the very end.

I VISITED MAGWITCH EVERY DAY BEFORE HIS TRIAL..

...you will be hanged by the neck until you are dead.

My Lord, I have received my sentence of death from the Almighty, but I bow to yours.

WHILE WAITING FOR THE SENTENCE TO BE CARRIED OUT, MAGWITCH BECAME MORE AND MORE ILL...

Are you in much pain today?

I don't complain of none, dear boy.

You never complain.

Dear Magwitch, I must tell you now, at last. You had a child once, whom you loved and lost. She lived, and found powerful friends. She is living now. She is a lady and very beautiful. And I love her.

He has gone. Oh Lord, be merciful to him, a sinner.

Sir, you are arrested. You owe money - one hundred and twenty-three pounds.

The police took all of Magwitch's money. How am I ever going to pay these bills?

He's too ill to be moved. We'll come back later.

I WAS SICK WITH WORRY.

Am I dreaming, or is it Joe?

That it is, old chap. Glad to see you're feeling a bit better.

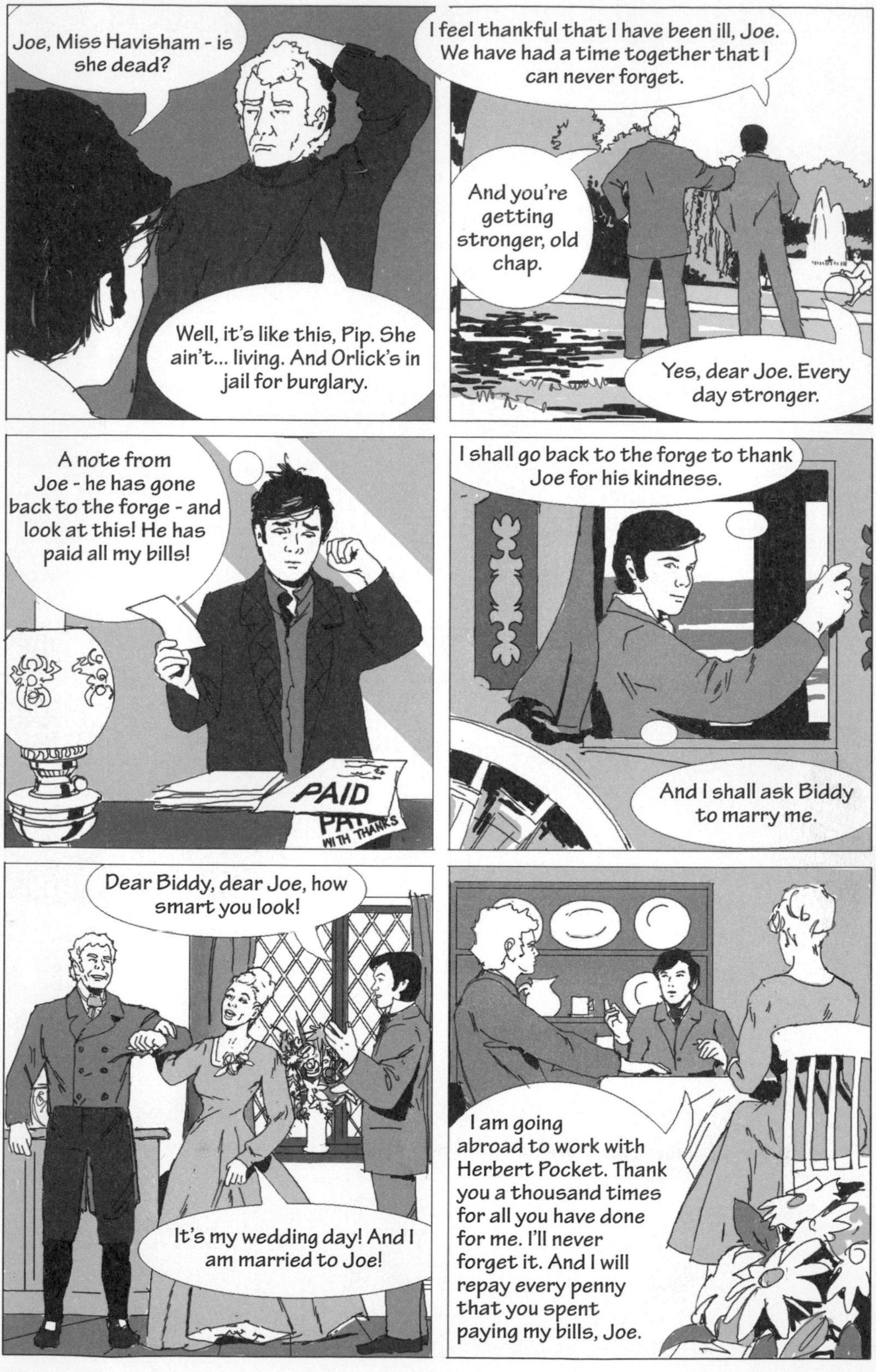

Joe, Miss Havisham - is she dead?
Well, it's like this, Pip. She ain't... living. And Orlick's in jail for burglary.
I feel thankful that I have been ill, Joe. We have had a time together that I can never forget.
And you're getting stronger, old chap.
Yes, dear Joe. Every day stronger.
A note from Joe - he has gone back to the forge - and look at this! He has paid all my bills!
PAID
PAID WITH THANKS
I shall go back to the forge to thank Joe for his kindness.
And I shall ask Biddy to marry me.
Dear Biddy, dear Joe, how smart you look!
It's my wedding day! And I am married to Joe!
I am going abroad to work with Herbert Pocket. Thank you a thousand times for all you have done for me. I'll never forget it. And I will repay every penny that you spent paying my bills, Joe.

IN THE MEANTIME, WEMMICK MARRIED MISS SKIFFINS.

HERBERT DID VERY WELL IN CAIRO.

I WAS VERY LONELY WITHOUT HIM.

AS SOON AS I WAS ABLE, I SOLD EVERYTHING AND JOINED HERBERT IN CAIRO.

BY WORKING HARD AND SAVING MY MONEY, I FINALLY REPAID THE MONEY I OWED TO JOE.

JUST FOUR MONTHS LATER, HERBERT AND CLARA WERE MARRIED.

ELEVEN YEARS LATER I RETURNED TO SEE BIDDY AND JOE.

And what about Estella, do you still miss her?

I heard she had an unhappy marriage, Biddy. Her husband beat her. He died in a riding accident two years ago. She has probably married again.

Estella!

I am greatly changed. I wonder you know me.

Life has not been easy. I have been bent and broken, but - I hope - into a better shape. Tell me we are friends.

We are friends. You have always held your place in my heart.

I TOOK HER HAND IN MINE, AND WE WENT OUT OF THE RUINED PLACE. AND AS THE MORNING MISTS HAD RISEN LONG AGO WHEN I FIRST LEFT THE FORGE, SO THE EVENING MISTS WERE RISING NOW, AND IN ALL THE BROAD EXPANSE OF TRANQUIL LIGHT THEY SHOWED TO ME, I SAW THE SHADOW OF NO PARTING FROM HER.